Library of Congress Cataloging-in-Publication Data

Vries, Anke de, 1936-
[Mijn olifant kan bijna alles. English]
My elephant can do almost anything / Anke de Vries ; paintings by
Ilja Walraven. -- 1st American ed.
p. cm.
Summary: The owner of a remarkable elephant proudly describes his
pet's feats, including balancing on the coffeepot, hanging from the
ceiling, and walking a tightrope.
ISBN 1-886910-06-5 (alk. paper)
[1. Elephants--Fiction. 1. Pets--Fiction.] I. Walraven, Ilja.
1959- ill. II. Title.
PZ7.V986My 1996
[E]--dc20 95-40267

Originally published in the Netherlands under the title:
Mijn olifant kan bijna alles by Lemniscaat b.v. Rotterdam

Printed and bound in Belgium
First American edition

My Elephant
Can Do Almost Anything

Anke de Vries

Paintings by Ilja Walraven

FRONT STREET & LEMNISCAAT

ARDEN, NORTH CAROLINA

My elephant can do almost anything.

He can stand on a wobbly stool,

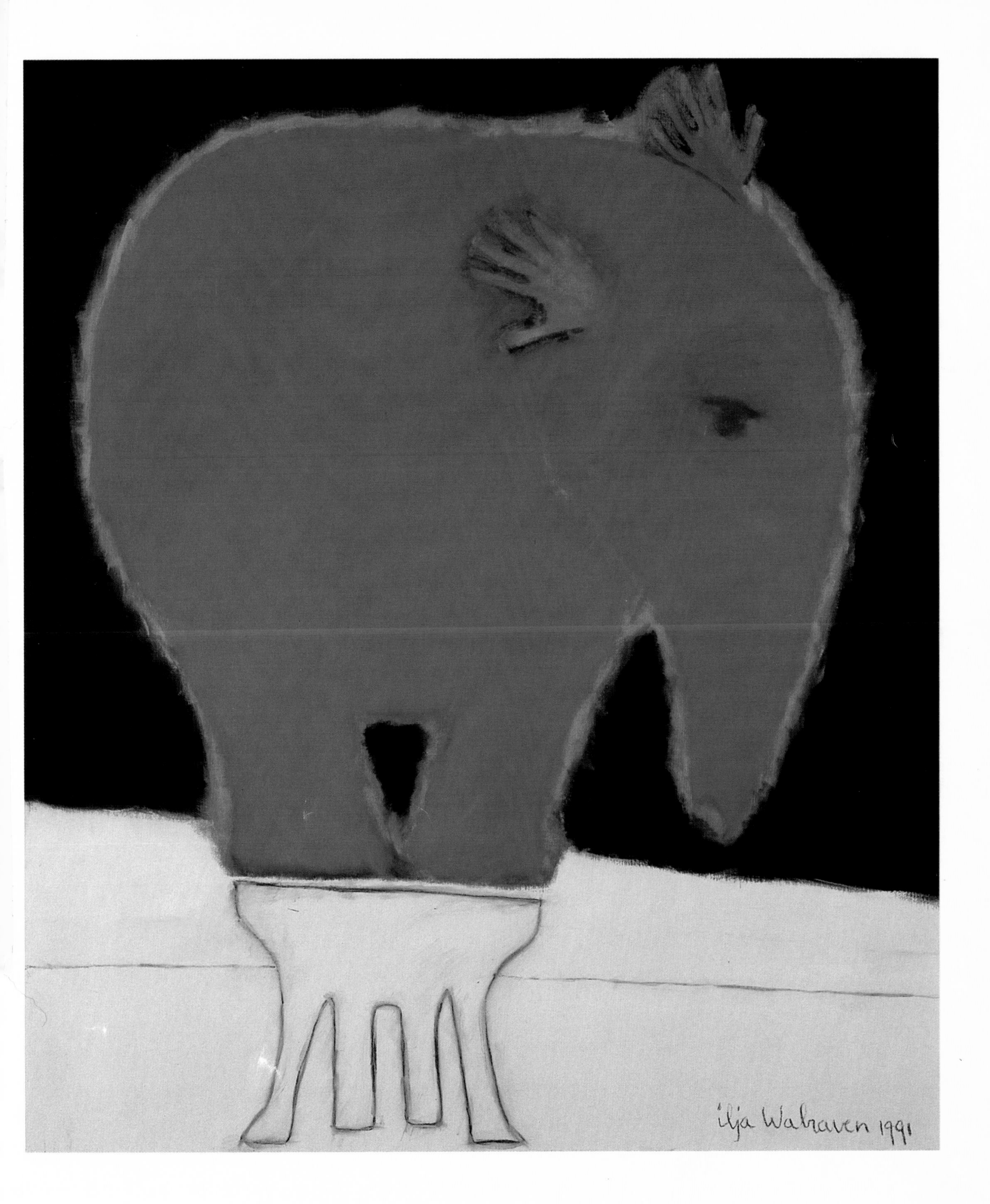
ilja Walraven 1991

and he can balance on a balloon.

Watch out! It will pop!

“Don’t worry,” my elephant says.

“As long as I hold my breath, I’m fine.”

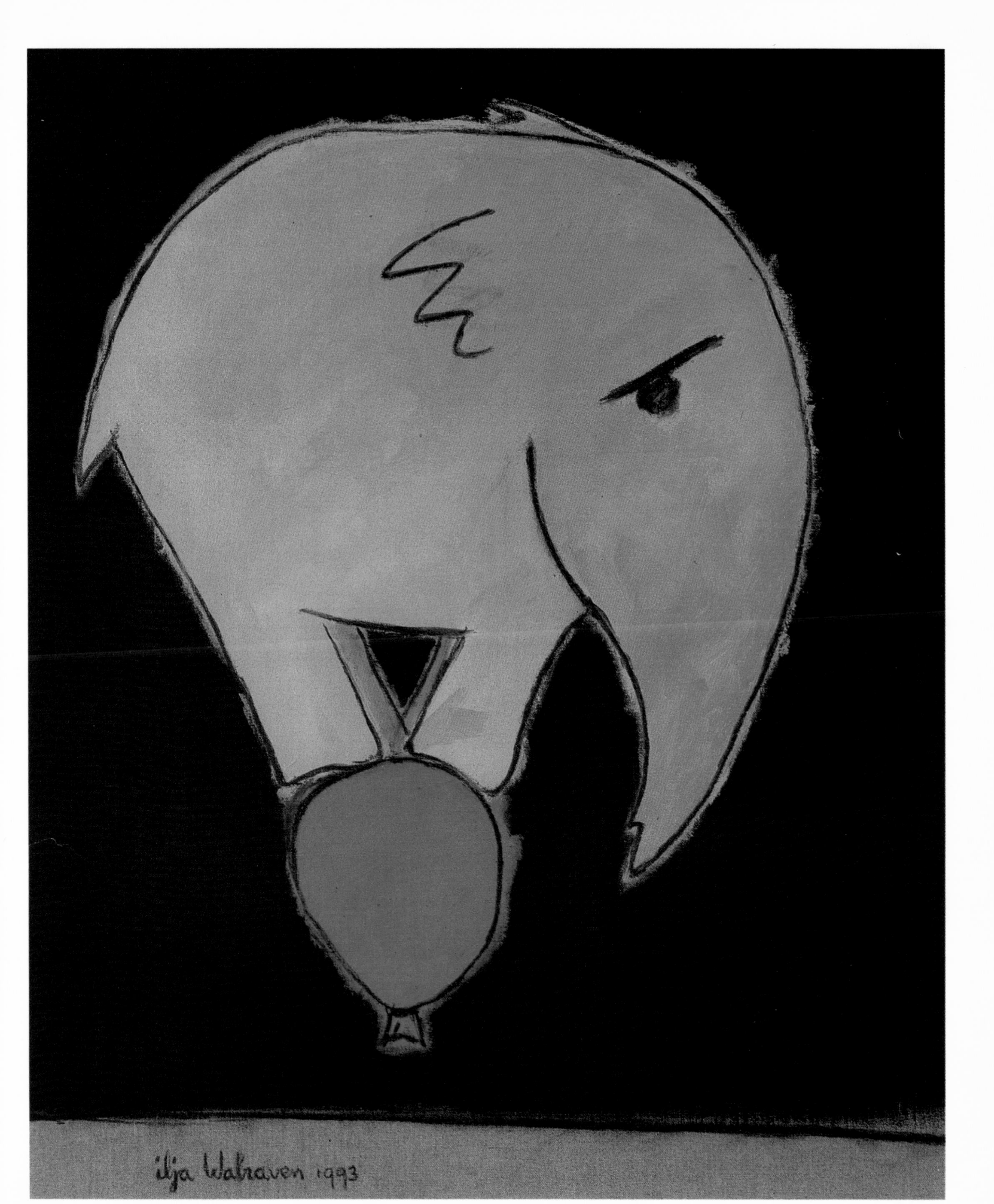
ilja Walraven 1993

The other day he even stood on top
of the coffeepot. “Look what I can do!”
But when Mom saw him
he had to get off, of course.

Sometimes he climbs up the wall
and hangs from the ceiling.
"Hello down there!" he says.

But when he tried to wave

he fell down. He wasn't hurt,

but I wrapped him up in bandages,

just in case.

He doesn’t like the bandages very much.

“They slow me down!” he says.

Now he is learning how to walk a tightrope

– very, very carefully.

When we play together

he always wants to get dressed up.

But we don't have any clothes his size,

so I paint him instead.

ilja Walraven 92/93

Today I painted him in stripes.

When he wiggles he looks like fire!

Everybody is scared stiff

– except me, of course.

ilja Walraven 1993

My elephant loves hats.

He wears a different one each day.

Some people have hats of every color.

My elephant changes colors for every hat.

At night he always wants to sleep with me,

but he's much too big.

"All right, all right, I'll get out."

He sleeps at the foot of my bed.

Ilja Walraven 1991

My elephant is never afraid of the dark.

He has special night eyes.

Even when it's pitch black he can see everything!

ilja Walraven 1992

He can even see through things.

When our cat walks across the room

he knows exactly what she had for supper.

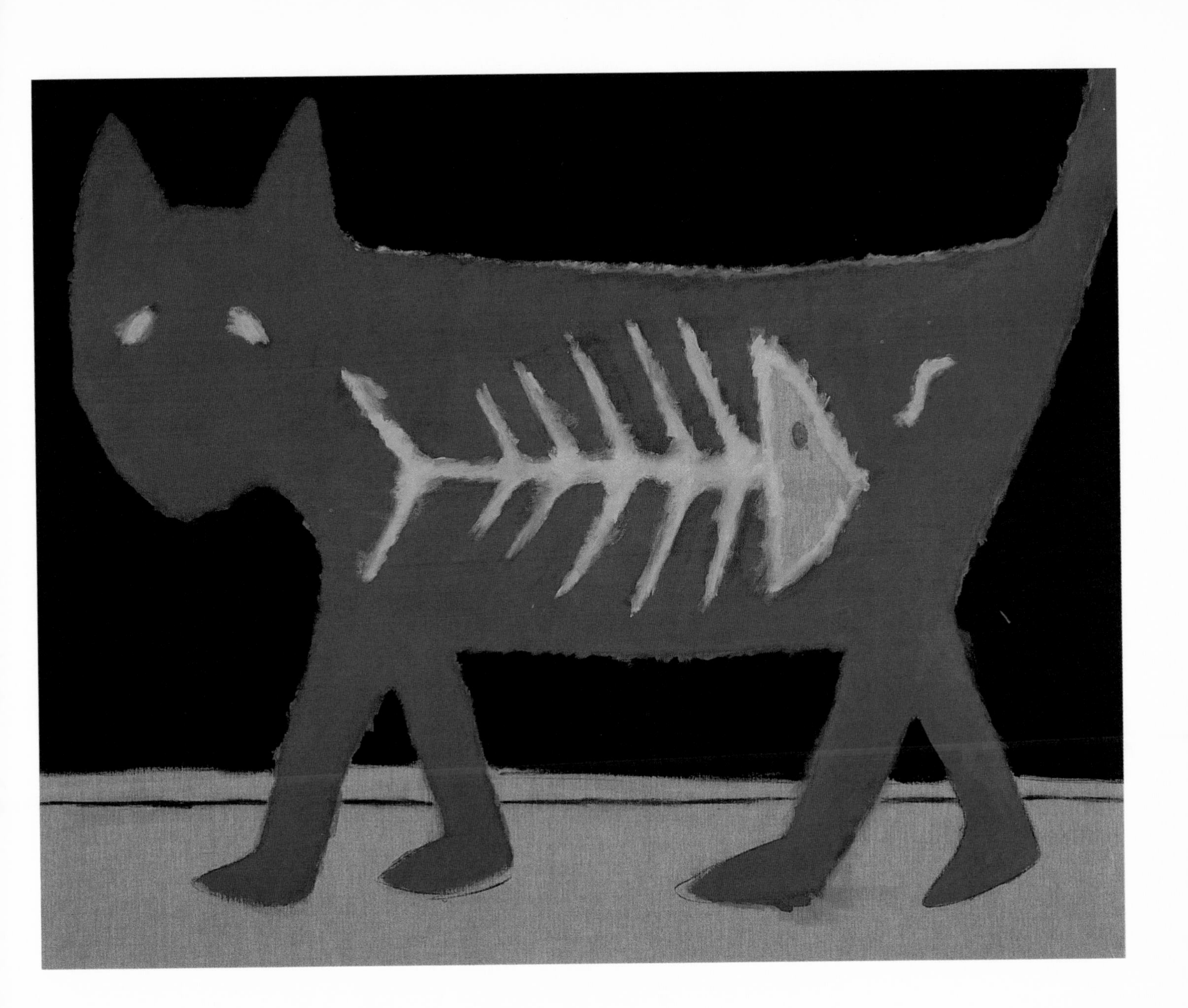

When I go to school my elephant is very sad.

He just stands in a corner and groans.

You can hardly recognize him.

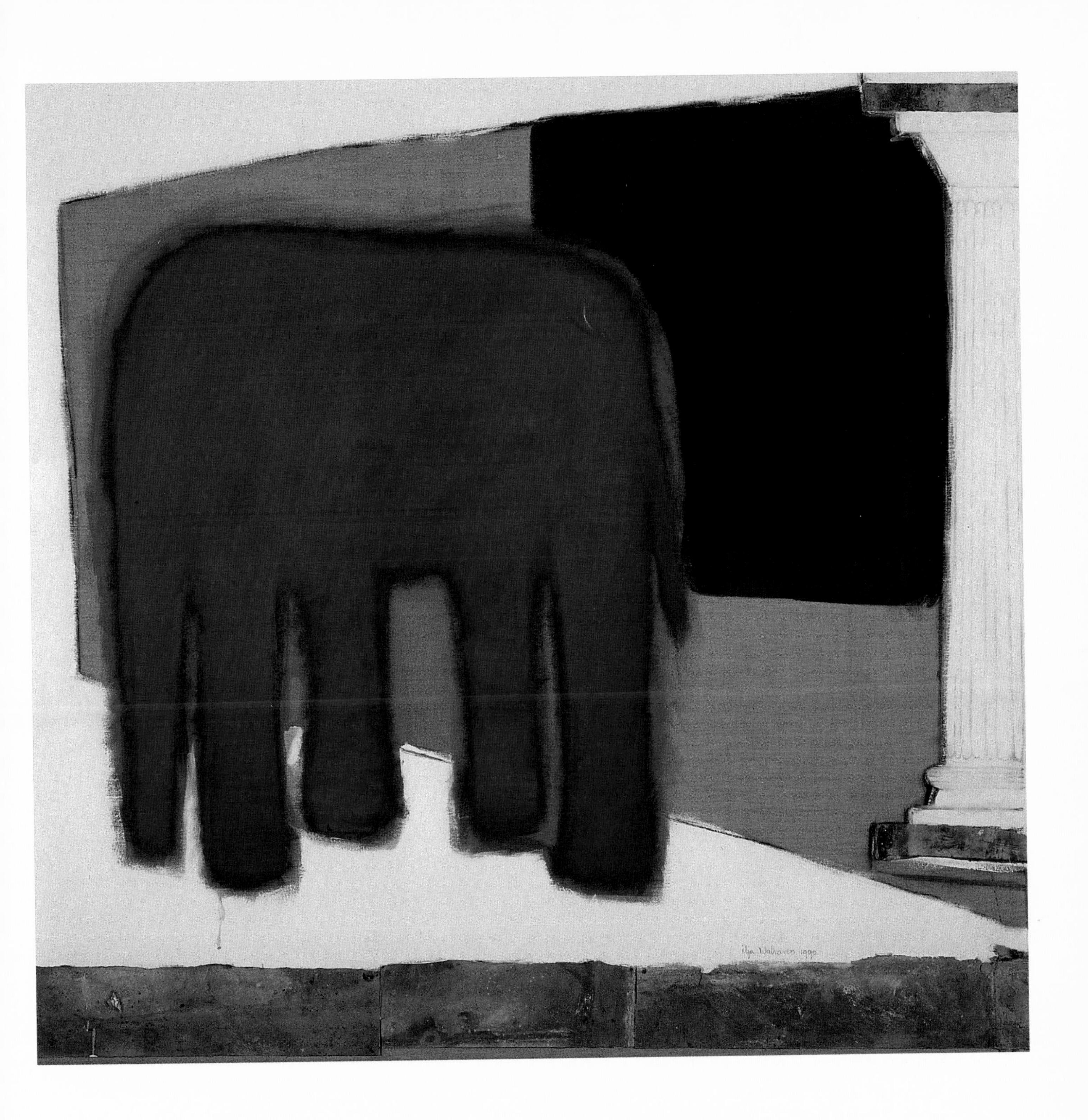
Ilja Walraven 1990

But when I come home again

he runs to meet me,

because there's one thing my elephant can't do...

he can't do without me!

Ceci n'est pas un pigeon